The Adventures

of Ear Z;

The Beginning

By Rashawn Epps

Copyright © Statement

No part of this book may be reproduced or transmitted in any form or by any means, electronic or mechanical, including recording, photocopying, or by any information storage and retrieval system, without the written permission of the publisher.

Fiction Statement

This is a work of fiction. Names, characters, places, and incidents are products of the authors' imaginations or are used fictitiously and are not to be construed as real. Any resemblance to actual events, locales, organizations, or persons, living or dead, is entirely coincidental.

Table of Contents

Chapter One

The Start of a Normal Day

I know you are wondering how I got like this, with the miniaturized Nike shoes, the bobblehead athletes, and cases of sprite. Although I am a rabbit, if you call me a bunny,

By Rashawn Epps

I cannot guarantee your safety. My name is Ear-Z and yes, I am a rabbit and this is my story.

Today was just like any other day, my alarm went off; however, this time it would change everything I knew, or would it? I used to think I was just like every other young rabbit, but I learned the hard way over the years; you live and learn right? I went into the kitchen expecting something to eat instead I found piles and piles of debris. Immediately, my mom came in the room and lost her fur. I was worried, but it was only a cave in. I thought my mom was going to have a heart attack. This had happened before so I knew I needed to patch and repair the hole before I could go anywhere.

I wanted to go meet up with my good friend Tito and meet my other friends at Green Pond. My Uncle Leroy and Big Bucky were going to be at the pond along with my friends Larry and Eddie from the chipmunk crew. My mom needed my help so I made sure everything was ok with the repair of the roof. After that was done, I worked on my chores, so I could go to meet up with my friends. Then my mom said, "If you must leave the house and go see your friends can you please watch out for strangers and the McLips. My friend Rosa said the McLips are out being wild and crazy and that the McLips were on the prowl for anyone in their area after night." I replied, "I know momma, and I will avoid that area. I will stay away from danger." I thought to myself, does my mom know something that I don't know? So out the door I went, down the path with woody orange towering trees with crispy grass and high rises.

Chapter Two

Danger! Watch Out!

The forest was thick, but the sun dappled through the trees. I went up a hill that looked never-ending, I passed the Blue Mountain that has a waterfall with a shooting fountain.

By Rashawn Epps

Today I was feeling good, other days I normally would take breaks and relax at the water but not today. Suddenly, I felt a sprinkle then I heard a roaring wind and thunder. It gave me the chills and I started getting cold, but I knew I was not a little bunny anymore and I could handle the situation. I figured I needed to get to cover, or find a place for shelter. The sky was darkening, and I was getting tired, but I was determined to withstand the cold and muggy conditions. As I looked around for shelter, I heard a loud roaring noise. I wondered what it could be. I zeroed in on the direction the noise was coming from and I moved in that direction. The noise was getting louder and becoming clearer. That could be a potentially dangerous situation for me should I stop or keep walking? I heard my mom's warning, but I am not a chicken and I decided to go forward. I heard a sharp loud noise and I became motionless. Up ahead, I saw a grove and Blackberry bushes, then I heard birds. Suddenly, out of the brush appeared two black birds cawing and a snake lunging toward them barely missing a bite. The snake then moved off in the direction of the birds. All of a sudden, I hear a faint voice saying, "Please help me, I am not going to make it." I moved

slowly but my legs felt like they were frozen. I

replied, "I cannot see through the darkness

and windy rain." Then the voice repeated

what it said before but this time, it sounded

different. So I replied again and said, "Where

are you!?" they sounded like it had a mouth

full of food, but I was thinking it couldn't be

that; I thought they could be hurt or in terrible

pain. My only option was to find out what was

going on and help if I could. As I moved

forward, I was aware of the trees and the

sounds of the forest, but I was mostly worried

about the snake. I finally made it to the brush,

and I dug, moved tree limbs, and twigs. Then I saw a squirrel it was not bleeding but it was stuck. The feet looked entangled and wrapped in vines. As I got closer I noticed it was Tito and his feet were pressed against a tree limb and his mouth was full of an orange round ball, and he had an orange powder around his mouth and all over his fingers. I removed the orange ball and he said, "Cheese balls mmm so tasty. Oh! Ear-Z, by the way we are in the McLips snake den and I am being used as bait for other animals, so we need to get out of here." I immediately wanted to leave, but I had to help. So, I asked Tito, "How did you get stuck here like this, I thought you were going to Green Pond? My momma said to watch out for the McLips, and now I am in the danger zone because of you!" He answered, "The snakes are using animals as bait, and you have to try these cheese balls. I don't like snakes but they are on to something with these cheese balls." He was stuffing so many cheese balls in his mouth that another orange ball was appearing before my eyes. Then, I heard some movement and a loud gaping sound and birds cawing. I started trying to unfree Tito the best I could as quickly as I could. Then, I heard the noise again, but this time the noise sounded much closer than before. Then, just as I am getting him free, the noise goes completely silent. I looked at Tito immediately to draw his attention and moved my head, hinting to him to get on my back. He was more concerned about getting more cheese balls. I yelled, "Snake!" Instantly, Tito darted towards me and wrapped his hands around my neck. At the same time, a reddish-colored snake came toward us. The snake started charging and, Tito could not stop screaming. With Tito on my back, I dashed in the direction in which I entered the den. I remembered I was on a mountain and I knew I was not as fast as a snake, and I could not tell if there were more than one. The fastest way down the mountain was straight down. The McLips were furious that their meal was getting away. We stumbled down the hill and luckily, I found a log, jumped on and gave it a little push down the hill. The McLips were coming fast and luckily, the log had a hole big enough for us to jump into. Turns out, there was more than one snake and they were coming after us. Some of the snakes got on the log, but were knocked off by trees and because of the extreme speed we were moving at. The snakes fell off the log and we continued moving rapidly down the mountain away from the danger. We both looked back, but the McLips had stopped chasing us. We were relieved, but we could not stop the momentum. We were picking up more and more speed. As we went off the cliff, I felt like we ran into something, but there was not anything there that I could see. Out of nowhere, I hear someone angrily shout, "Ouch!" Tito and I had flown out of the log, and as we were falling a frog magically appeared in front of me. The frog was not falling, it looked like it was hovering. The look it was giving me made my stomach ache. Before I knew it, Tito and I had landed in the river, making a big splash. Once I got my head out of the water I noticed a spaceship was parked on the cliff of the mountain. Meanwhile, Janus (the frog I ran into), had it out for me from that point on. After I fell into the water he was angry and enraged and watched from afar to learn more about me. He then went back to his spaceship and told the other members on his team about what had happened to him. Janus was courageous, and he was honorable but sometimes his temper got the best of him. His second in command was an ape named Mascow Dubbaca, but he could only communicate by sign language and the only thing he could say verbally was his name. Janus would commonly finish his thoughts and look towards Mascow Dubbacca for his opinion. Janus rushed back to his ship and told his crew that he had been assaulted and that he wanted revenge on the rabbit. He said that the earth creatures had no respect for higher beings and he wanted them to assimilate into their culture to find out more about the species living on this planet.

Meanwhile back to me, I was struggling for air and I was terrified, but I was not going to give up. I saw the log floating in the water, and I managed to grab ahold of it. Tito was not on the log, I yelled out to him but I didn't hear anything back. I looked around in both directions in a panic worried for Tito. Then I saw him ahead of me in the water floating. He was alive, but I could not reach him. Then he vanished, and I yelled out his name, and I immediately noticed there was a waterfall ahead. I tried to paddle in the other direction, but it was not working. I tried using both of my paws in the water to go in the other directions, but the current was too strong. I went over the waterfall and I yelled, "Tito!"

Chapter Three

New Horizons

I woke up feeling dizzy and foggy. Somehow, I was still alive and I knew it was not because of me. The last thing I remembered was going over a waterfall. I noticed Tito sleeping next me, and there were yellow flowers and daises everywhere. Then I heard a voice, it was a voice I had never heard before; it was soft and angel like. I spotted a brown bunny with white marks on her fur, she was absolutely mesmerizing. I asked her, "Who are you and where am I?" She replied, "I am Abir, and you are welcome." Confused, I ask, "You are welcome for what I just met you." Then she replied, "I pulled you and your friend out of the river yesterday, and that you are welcome to stay here. You can grab some food and something to drink, but my friends and I are playing baseball. I said,

"What is baseball?" She replied, "It is a human sport we learned, and we love it. If you want to give it a try come join us if you want to play." I was hesitant to respond then I heard Tito say, "I'll play, what are you waiting for." I had never played baseball before and Tito was eager. Then I heard someone yell, "Heads up, watch out for the ball!" Then I felt a sharp thump on my head. The ball had struck me on my forehead. It knocked me to the ground then I heard Abir say, "Are you okay? How is your head? You should rest up until you feel well enough to travel." Befuddled, I replied, "I am fine, I will be okay! Tito, we have to go.

Our friends are probably worried and still waiting for us at the pond."

Back on the path I had to ask Tito how he got tangled up with the snakes. He told me that he saw that the snakes had just found food and he thought he would wait until they went to sleep to go steal some. But instead of just taking some food, he had other plans. He spotted a snake with really big lips, and he could not resist the urge to flick them. Turns out those big lips belonged to the momma snake. This made the other snakes wake up and threatened to eat him but luckily, they put him in the trap because the snakes had recently eaten. He said it was an accident, but the McLips did not believe him. Knowing Tito and his personality who knows what his real intensions were. Either way, I was happy to have my friend safe and alive. Tito talked about his family and how he was the youngest of three brothers. He talked about all his second-place prizes and how hard it was for him not to be number one, or picked first. He told me about how his brothers got him second place ribbons for his birthdays and keep number 2 pencils in his room. He told me everything about the first time he beat someone up. He said he won his first fight, but he was left with two black eyes. Some of it was entertaining, but most of it was over the top. I decided I had enough, so I told him to zip it! He looked at me and immediately started laughing. This is why we are good friends.

Chapter Four

Green Pond

Finally, we started to approach Green Pond I was very happy to see that everyone was there. Some were all playing in the water having a good time there were others on lily pads and house boats and it looked lively. We ran as fast as we could and jumped in, splashing each other. It was amazing I finally got to my friends and we were having so much fun! My friends in the Chipmunk Crew, Larry and Eddie were easily spotted. I then located my friend Harry the Raccoon and Dennis the guinea pig sitting on the edge of a big rock talking with Larry and Eddie, those boys are wild!

I remember one time I saw Eddie or maybe it was Larry messing with a big monkey; Larry is a chipmunk, what was he going to do against a monkey? The monkey was not bothering Larry, but Larry was throwing nuts at the monkey from up in the tree and hitting him on the head. Then when the monkey looked to see who threw them, Larry would go hide. After a while, Eddie would sneak down by the monkey and steal some of his food. This made the monkey very angry, because he could not see who was doing it. Those chipmunks were working with ants to acquire food. Their plan was to have Eddie and Larry distract the monkey, so the ants could sneak away with the food. Then there was my friend Slow Pete, he was a salamander. He is never on time, but when he shows up he is funny and over the top. He always talked about how lizards are making a comeback in the world. He told me that strangers had arrived at the pond a few days ago, and that there were seven of them. He told me they were frogs, but they were not really frogs. He told me that they came from the stars and that although they were different they had similar qualities like us. He went on to describe each of the frogs and told me a little about what he knew about each of them. Slow Pete told me that he saw a rabbit change into a frog, but I didn't believe. He went on to tell me that there were seven visitors at the pond that came from the stars. He said that they came from a planet that was near Saturn many days ago. However, they were on Earth and they were far from ordinary; they could fly, talk and adapt to different languages, and transform into anything. Lilly was their leader. Then there was Abir, her eyes could capture any animal's heart, and she had mine, but I was too afraid to say anything. Maybe I was nervous at the time, but I couldn't stop looking in Abir's direction, so I went over to talk to her. Tito abruptly said, "We have a problem there are three frogs and a very large ape coming towards us, how do you want to handle this Ear-Z?" Janus asked me and Tito, "Why are you talking to my girl? Then Abir responded immediately in a loud voice, "I am not your girl, don't get it twisted". Just as that happened Janus appeared to be enraged and he directed his frustration towards Ear-Z. Janus said, "Look up" and pointed towards a tree then immediately slapped Ear-Z. Janus and his friends began to laugh along with other animals at the pond. He then said he saw a bug on Ear-Z then flung himself towards Ear-Z and he accidentally hit me across the face. Janus was not always bad, he had good qualities and he was a warrior for his people.

Janus was powerful and demanding and sometimes two-faced when his emotions were stirred. He was also the protector of Abir, and the commander of the Forgorian Tribe, a group of alien warriors. Mascow Dubacca was a large ape but he was kind, gentle, and was always fair. He appeared to be an open-minded individual. He was very friendly with all the frogs but fiercely loyal to Janus. He was understanding and caring to the other animals who came to the pond. Then there was Hector. Now this frog had something wrong with his voice, but he appeared to be rounder than the others and you can generally find him eating. I

always wondered about his voice, he could
have just been sick, but it sounded like he had
a fly in his throat. Hector often used gadgets
and was very smart, you could tell he was not
from here. Then there was Chad, he was
unlike the others. He was creative and diverse,
and had more powers than the others. If Chad
became over-excited and lost his focus he
would shoot rays of destruction from his eyes.
With time he would learn how to control it,
but he was young and his time would come.
He was still young and mainly followed the
advice of Abir and Hector. Then there was
Tania she was wild and fierce, her courage

was unchallenged, and her beauty was unmatched. She generally had something witty to say when she was approached by an advancing male. She would say the same thing, "You can't touch this." Generally, when this would happen she would become very annoyed and wanted whoever was bothering her to leave her alone.

Everybody I knew was at Green Pond, even wild creatures and cocky unknown animals. Even some of my own relatives were there. I spotted my uncle Leroy Bunny and his friend, Big Bucky. They were headed in my direction. My uncle told me that my mom was supposed to be coming here, and that she was upset with me for not coming home last night. Then I heard my name being yelled, "Ear-Z, I see you! Bring your little bunny self over here!" I pretended like I didn't hear anything, and my uncle Leroy began talking about how important it was for us rabbits to stick together. Then he told me how my mom had been eating Green Pond carrots and how much she has been learning. The water from green pond has been said to improve your learning capabilities and heightened your senses. One drink of green pond water and you were forever changed. I began to realize there is a lot of stuff about my mother that I don't know. I see Abir and other rabbits playing in the water. Abir looks up and catches me looking at her, and smiles at me. I want to go over to her, but I can't get away from motor mouth. Tito is looking at me rubbing his stomach then says, "What are we going to eat?" I turned to Tito and tell him rapidly, "Go get your own food." Then I hear a loud yell, "Ear-Z run get out of here!" Then loud noises, sirens and green smoke clouded the area. The smoke was suffocating I heard screaming from all directions, then I saw humans coming closer and closer. The last thing I saw was Abir being grabbed, then it

was black.

Chapter Five

Captured!

I do not know how long I was knocked out. I woke up in a cage with other rabbits, some of the rabbits I knew but others I did not. From what I could tell there were a lot of animals from Green Pond that were caged except the members of the Forgorian Tribe.

Meanwhile, back at the pound Janus and Lilly were in a heated discussion about whether they were going to help the animals who had been captured. Lilly wanted to use their resources to get the captured animals out but Hector feared it would draw attention if they used their technology. Janus saw this struggle as an opportunity to gain power and take over the tribe. Janus stressed that Earth was the safest place in the solar system for them to be right now. With limited supplies the universe was not safe for them.

Meanwhile, I woke up in a cage, dizzy and disoriented. It looked like these humans in White Coats had been capturing animals for quite some time. It was a hard adjustment from being in the forest with my mom and friends then being cold in a cage surrounded by glass and strangers. I was trapped, and I felt alone and helpless. I thought about my mother and how she was doing and that she would want me to be strong, and not be scared.

I didn't know where my mom was, but I figured she was in another part of the facility. I could see my uncle and Big Bucky and I could also see some squirrels and chipmunks in cages nearby. I did not see Tito, or any of my other friends on those first few days. From what I could tell they were arranging the animals around by their levels of hostility and need.

I did not want to show weakness to the others, I wanted to remain a positive image for them. But at night when I laid down, so many nights my heart pounded faster than I could run. My tears drenched my fur, and I cried myself to sleep. There were other animals in other cages that I did not recognize and I knew that they did not come from my forest. Every morning before the sun rose, they would inject the animals with a blue serum. The injections made some of the animals go crazy, and made others act out of character. Some animals could handle it, but it made others go insane. When the animals became too wild or violent the White Coats would send them to the restricted area. There was a lot of security for that part of the facility. I did not know much about the restricted area, but I knew when animals went in there they never made it back out. There was gossip that the most powerful of animals were held in the restricted area. The animals that they did the secret test on were in there. Harry and Dennis spotted very large animals going into the restricted area unconscious. They passed messages that spread throughout the facility. Harry and Dennis gossiped and picked at each other just like brothers would. Although they came from different backgrounds they were banded together. Harry is an out-spoken nonconfrontational Raccoon, but he loves the colors yellow and purple. Dennis is a loud-mouthed Guinea pig that charges into the situation rather than thinking first.

All the animals were tested for improved intelligence and had supplements mixed into the food. They started with a small test, and then gradually worked their way to more intense tests. They used games to build teamwork and encouraged games like red light green light and freeze tag. They also took notes on how well we listened and tested our pain tolerance. At night the White Coats would display pictures of other animals and force us to watch television and educational learning tools. However, not all the White Coats treated us like experiments. Donna Flowers was a white coat and she was kind and gentle and taught the animals the games Red light green light and freeze tag. Animals that had not known each other where interacting with each other and forgetting their problems for a moment. It was told that the Rat King enjoyed playing red light green light with Donna Flowers. The animals changed over time after learning so much of human culture. Some remained the same, true to themselves, but others changed.

Chapter Six

Time for a Change

I knew I was a prisoner, but I knew I needed to learn more about the humans. So, as they studied us I studied them. I began to talk to the other Rabbits I knew in my cage however, they would not all talk to me, but I knew someone who could get them to listen, my uncle Leroy. My Uncle Leroy was the kind of Rabbit that if you give him a problem to fix he will solve it. He didn't always handle his problems the best way, but his method whether it looked normal or unorthodox was highly effective.

I knew I needed to learn more about the humans and that animals would have to be united if we were going to survive this.

Meanwhile everything changed when Donna Flowers transferred to a new job. When Donna left it caused problems that changed the facility. The rats were learning and progressing at a fast rate. The Rats were led by King Sunny, and he would direct the rats to attack the handlers or have the rats resist doing the test. Not all the rats would survive the test and the injections day after day. There were thousands of rats and they were intelligent and once they figured out that their injections improved the brain. The Rats that survived, they banded together and removed the weak. They had become organized, so The White Coats decided to hire janitors because they wanted to rotate the animals for new testing and they needed more workers to compete this task. The janitors would be hired as security and cleaners, but the janitors did not look like the White Coats at all. The White Coats had tan or pale skin and when they came in they were predictable. However, some of the janitors had brown skin and dark skin and some and had unknown color of skin. Since the rats were causing so many problems the White Coats started rotating animals every few days so we could not get to comfortable or plan, or attempt an escape. This was a good thing for the animals because news traveled a lot faster now that there were rotations. The janitors were required to watch us at night and maintain order. But at night we got to watch television and listen to music. This wasn't the kind of television we watched with the White Coats, the janitors would change the channel. We also learned about sports and American day time television. We learned that Kobe was better than Jordan from Eddy Carter. He would watch Laker games on the television and talk about the game as he did his work. Dennis and Harry would antagonize Eddy if his team was losing on occasion. Dennis would say, "Those Lakers aren't playing good today." then Harry would chime in, "I know number 24 is not playing good today." Then

Dennis asked," Where is the game at?" Harry replied," New York!" Then Dennis's mood changed and with great emotion said, "He always plays good in New York at the Garden." Sometimes Eddie appeared to be teary eyed when the Lakers lost a game. He would frequently yell out loud and he would often throw objects. He would emphatically throw objects in the direction of cages. He had other qualities that were different than the others, we learned about music and modern culture. If Eddy Carter was not watching the Lakers he was watching reruns of The Marvin Show every night. At first, I did not understand how making fun of your friends, and doing practical jokes on them would be acceptable and funny. How could he watch this kind of a show? As I watched the show for the first time I noticed a man the same color as Eddy, but he didn't act like the White Coats. He was funny and he dressed up in strange clothes and played different roles throughout the television show. I learned that not all humans are the same. Some people are different, and others may say things differently and look strange but that does not mean they are bad. I learned something new about human culture every time I watched

The Marvin Show. Because we were being rotated throughout the facility, I was learning more from each janitor I observed. I tried to keep up with everyone that I could.

I found Tito, and I located Abir, they were as safe as they could be. Over time, everyone that was caged became closer and closer. Animals that I thought were strange, were not so strange anymore. We were referred to as numbers I was number 425b and all the animals were tagged with their own numbers. I made it a point to talk to as many other animals as I could and that was made easier by the rotations. I wanted to talk to the other caged animals because our freedom was taken

but we were not defeated, and needed to have

hope. I wanted to explain to the others that the

humans were not our enemy. Our enemy is

their ambitions, and their fear of what they do

not understand. Not all the animals were

cooperating, there were some that were

defiant. King Sunny knew that the snakes

were feared by many, but he was not scared of

a snake. He knew this could be an advantage.

He knew that he needed to have a substitute

just in case the snake got hungry. He knew the

numbers and that there was more Rats than

there were snakes. He also knew the

disadvantages of the snake and that they didn't have hands to open doors. He also knew that if given the chance the snakes will likely try to eat him. He devised a plan in which he would never be alone with the snakes and he would send others in his place just in case the snakes had a change of heart, or got hungry.

He then offers a deal to the momma snake; he will supply them food, if they give him protection while in this place. The rats and the snakes were causing problems in the rotations. I was grateful that the snakes and rats were causing problems, because this allowed most of the animals to be rotated throughout the facility. The humans did not want the animals to get to comfortable in their new homes. This made it easy to find my friends and make sure that they were okay. I wanted to unify all the animals so we could limit injuries and wrongful deaths. But there was a problem I could not get to the Rat king. I knew if I could unite the animals we would have a better chance at some of us making it through this. Each day was hard and draining, but it was a stepping stone to a better day. My options were to stay trapped, or escape. Everyone I knew was caged and being monitored. Could I escape by myself and really leave them? I really didn't want to leave anyone behind and I had not located my mom yet. I knew I was going to need help, and I knew me just asking my friends were not going to be enough. I decided I would learn about all the janitors and I would pick one of them to help us. If I was going to risk talking to a human, I had to be sure to pick the correct one. I did not want to be on a table, and have more humans poking or running more test on me. I knew I needed to get a message to the Rat King. So, I needed a messenger I sent a message to my uncle Leroy to find Tito, and have him go talk to Rat king. For me to do this, I was going to have to get the power shut off, so Tito could get to Rat king. I knew I was risking my life, but I felt that I had no choice but to do something. I began to take notice to which janitors could be helpful and which janitors would not. There were a lot of janitors, but four of them stood out the most. The first one that stood out was Jorge, he was big and tall and was always smiling and dancing. I often saw him playing around and he didn't look to serious and helpful. Then next was Bobby she was very helpful and kind, but not when her teams are playing I wouldn't recommend saying anything bad about them. She also helped maintain our area, she kept it clean and I can appreciate that however, I wasn't sure if she would join our cause and help us. For the next few weeks I waited for a message from Tito. When the news finally came that the Rat King wanted dance off to settle who is in charge. He figured he was a superior animal and with his skills he could out dance or out smart any animal. I knew I had one chance to get this right, and I was going to risk everything. I decided that I was going to speak to a janitor and persuade one of them to help us. For days I thought about ways to get to the

Rat King. Then one day after the White Coats left I heard a phone ring it happened to be one of the janitor's personal phones. I heard one of the janitors say, "My baby's momma is sucking me dry, like Dracula. I am trying to do right by my son, but my checks are small. After she gets her money, I barely can afford to get a cheeseburger. Then when she allows me to see my son, when I get a day off, my son says dad, where is the milk and cookies? Isn't that something? Now I feel bad for hiding my milk and cookies." Bobby walks in the room and says, "Shawn, did you drink my chocolate milk?" Shawn replies, "No. I did not drink your chocolate milk buddy. Did you see a six

of purple soda in the breakroom?" Bobby

replied, "First of all, yes I did see it and

second, I am a female, just because I dress the

way I do, does not mean you can call me

buddy. I assume the grape soda is yours

Shawn?" Shawn replied, "Yes, it is mine, and I

did not drink your chocolate milk. You better

go ask one of the workers in the cafeteria, if I

was you I would go ask one of the other

janitors because I am not the one who did it."

Then Bobby walked off and went towards the

women's bathroom. I knew this was my best

chance to get help. When the words came out I

was not expecting them to be so loud because I have never spoken to a human before. In a high-pitched voice, I said, "Did you drink the chocca?" Shawn looked around startled and shouted, "Who said that! Show yourself!" Then I said it again, and he zoomed his eyes in on me and began to walk slowly towards my cage. He replied, "No I did not drink the chocolate milk." He then turned his back to me and began talking to himself and I was worried for a bit. I told him that the animals needed help and we needed him to help us. He immediately told me no, he would not help me. That he was not going to risk his job for a silly rabbit that can talk. I told him my name was Ear-Z, and that I'm not a silly rabbit. Then I asked him, "Where are we? How can we help you, so you can help us?" He replied, "You are in a cage at the Dulce Laboratory, and you are being watched. How could you possibly help me?" I told him that I was a lot smarter and tougher than I looked. I asked him, "Will you help us? We could help you with your money problem." He replied, "How can you help me with money if you are just a rabbit?" I told him that yes, I was rabbit, but I could talk to other animals and that we could get things done. I told him I needed to get a message to the outside and that we could secure some money. I told him about how the rats were causing problems and how I needed to get Tito to the rats. I told him that I needed him to turn off the power and maybe unlock a cage or two. He looked at me, his eyes were big, and then he said he could not set us free in a soft voice. He said he would try to help us but suddenly an alarm went off and Shawn abruptly took off running out the door.

By Rashawn Epps

Chapter Seven

New Arrivals, More Troubles

Meanwhile, at the entrance of the Dulce, some White Coats were coming through the gates, pushing carts with more animals in cages. The noises were sharp, the moment brought fear, and you could hear voices but you could not see the animals. They were moving the new animals to the restricted area and even the janitors were not allowed in there. The White Coats pushed the carts along the hallways stopping only to tag the cages. They begin the process of tagging the animals before they headed to the restricted area. One of the cages tipped over and they had captured more rabbits and then it happened, a voice yelled, "Ear-Z! Help, please help! Find my son!" The words echoed throughout the facility and all of the animals began whispering. The White Coats abruptly put the cage back on the cart and continued the process. After they finished tagging the animals the White Coats pushed the cart towards the restricted area. To get to the restricted area, they had to go past the rats and snakes. There was a code that the White Coats used to get into the restricted area, and the rats were in a perfect position to see that code.

Ear-Z did not know anything about what was going on, the news had not reached him yet. He had heard the loud alarm from another part of the building. He knew what that meant: there was a problem in the facility. It was a very long night and I was worried that

Shawn would talk to White Coats or do something or even worse. Some of the animals were saying that I doomed us. So I had to think of a plan to ensure our survival.

I knew they were studying ants and I knew they could get a message outside. I was thinking even if I could find a way to get an ant on the outside, could I trust an ant? They are fickle, and they have beady little eyes. I don't know any ants, but I had friends who did. I remembered Eddie and Larry were very close to the ants. I had a lot of thoughts in my head and I was worried about my mom and how she was. I needed to devise a plan to get the ants on the outside to collect money for Shawn. I also needed Tito to go to the Rat King and accept his challenge so the animals could be united. I had not heard anything from Shawn in days, because of the rotations and his work schedule. I also worried if he would keep my secret, or betray me. My mind was clouded, and I began to worry.

Minutes turned into hours, and soon days turned to weeks. Then to my surprise Shawn decided to help us, but he said he would require payment before he would help us escape. There was still the issue of the Rat King and the dance off. I had to figure out a way to get Shawn to help us, and then I remembered Eddy Carter was always watching the Marvin Show; I thought to myself, what would Marvin do if he were in a cage? The answer to that hit me like a lightning bolt. That was easy he would keep talking and he would not give up until he completed his mission. In the show, Marvin did a lot of talking but he never turned on his friends. He would help his friends if he could, he even helped the awkward and strange characters on in his TV show. I began to think, if I could be a good friend and do what Marvin did I could get out of here and I could help everybody. I decided I was going to use my voice more and I was going to get my animal family to help me. I sent messages cage by cage, with a goal in mind that it would reach the ants in the coming days. Getting a message to another animal was a tricky situation. Sometimes you would have to wait for the rotation shifts because it was hard to directly communicate. The message was simple, I wanted them to be informed about the coming events but getting a message to them was going to be difficult because they were located near the restricted area. I got a message to Big Bucky and Tito that we would be heading to the Rat King soon and to be prepared for anything. For the next few days I thought how I was going to proceed.

Chapter Eight

There might be hope

Meanwhile the other animal's whispers of what happened about Ear-Z's mother had reached Tito's ears. However, Tito was on a mission of his own and he was attempting to steal some food from the White Coats. He heard other animals discussing a terrible scene a mother enslaved and yelling for her son. Tito knew he was going to have to dance and he needed more energy to practice and that required food. He had to get his moves right and he had to be number one not number two. Eddy and Larry were coaching Tito on his dance moves in the cages, getting his water and helping him acquire more food. While Tito was focused on improving his dancing, I was focused on a plan to escape. I wanted to escape, but it was not practical that all of the animals would get out on the first attempt. I formulated a plan to have the animals that were located by the janitor Eddy Carter introduce themselves and to try not to scare him. With this plan there was a risk, but I figured that it was more likely that he would help us. I just had a feeling that he would. For the next few nights the animals located by Eddy began to slowly introduce themselves. During The Marvin Show, the animals would yell out and dance to his music. They were very private animals until they learned about music and dance. The guinea pig Dennis was very outspoken, he would make jokes to get a laugh from him. Dennis and Harry always managed to get located right by one another.

The wild raccoon was impulsive, and he did

not like confrontations, but he liked to watch

TV and make jokes. He would ask Eddy about

his personal life and what it was like being

human. Eddy was nervous at first talking to

animals, but it became second nature to him,

and he kept our secret. For most of the animals

during the day it was hard to smile but at

night the janitors made it easier, with their

smiles and kind spirts and openness to us not

just wanting to take from us or harm us.

The day that our lives changed began like

any other day. It started with testing and being

poked and instructed to do things. It was hard to be tested and monitored and in harsh conditions. The constant state of being hungry then being relocated or subjected to a new location by force. The rats were led by King Sunny who created an empire wherever he was. But he could dance like no other, his moves were flamboyant and his words could make or end you. His minions were the snakes. They were just as unpredictable, but they had a code they went by. The snakes and the rats created a dynamic tension among the animals because they promoted dominance and disorder. They did not care for abiding guidelines. They only cared about what benefited them. That day I heard no noises, but the day felt longer than others. The darkness set in and moon beams were shooting through the windows. The janitors appeared, and I saw Shawn coming my way, but he wasn't deviating from his course. He was coming straight towards me. He came close enough to my cage and said, "My plans have changed, tonight is your night, let me know when you need the power off." He moved in the other direction like nothing had happened. I then thought to myself if he turned off the power right away there would be drama and dysfunction, because all the animals would be out of their cages. If I sent a message and it fell into the wrong hands (like the rats) it could become a disadvantage, the rats could formulate their own plan. Their control of other animals by fear and their control of other sectors should not be taken lightly. I wanted to be well prepared for when Shawn came back. I sent a message to Tito, Big Bucky, and Uncle Leroy to be prepared for the unexpected and that tonight was the night.

By Rashawn Epps

Chapter Nine

Free at last

When Shawn finally came back into my sector he looked at me and I looked at him and nodded. Then moments later the power was off. You could hear grunts, yells and voices. I could hear cheering, shouts and loud noises. There were sounds of glass being broken and an alarm was going off and red lights flickering. The lights in the room instantly shut off, and the room became dark, the only lights were green lower lights with dust clouds. I was nervous seeing and witnessing these events, but I knew I had to act fast. I made my way out of my cage to a cold and unfamiliar ground. My plan was to get to the Rat King, unite the animals, and escape. There was a problem: when I got to the floor I saw a crowd of animals by the door. They could not open the door. The humans had created push button doors, and they were too far up for anyone to reach. Big Bucky was strong, and I told him to grab a chair and move it by the door. He looked at me and said, "How about you do it Ear-Z, you got the brains." Then Tito said, "We can all help." So, we moved the chair by the door. Just as we managed to get the chair to the door Shawn appeared and opened the door and asked, "Do you need help?" As he opened the door we all fell on the floor. Tito said, "Now that's how you make an entrance." We all laughed, and then got ourselves up. I didn't want to involve Shawn any more than I already had so I told him to go to the ants and tell them to escape through the sewers and to get help. I told him to tell them to go through the sewers because of the green fog and I knew what it could do. Shawn told us that the Rats and snakes had come together with the wolves to form a blockade in sector 15, which was located near the restricted area. Shawn also said that wolves were devouring the animals that wouldn't join them, or make them run in terror. The rats had tapped into the computer security system for the facility. I knew going forward things would be difficult, and I knew that I had to do something for my friends to survive because some animals could not fight for themselves. Going down the hallway Big Bucky was out ahead checking each corner looking for threats. Each step I felt could be my last, but I was not going to stop. As we arrived at a door, we were greeted with growls and a deep voice saying, "Why are you here?" We all looked at each other thinking, what is going on and then a rat appeared. We look down and laughed then the rat spoke, but this time the voice was obviously not coming from the rat. Two wolves were behind him. One was big, with golden brown and white fur, and his mouth opened showing his teeth. The other was bigger with black fur and blue eyes. The wolves appeared behind the rat and we stopped laughing immediately. Once we stopped laughing we heard another voice, but this time it was quiet. The rat said, "What do you have to say now? It's not so funny now. Go ahead and laugh at me some more." Big Bucky replied, "We are here for the dance off with the King." The wolf with black fur said, "Follow me." We entered sector 15 and all the cages were opened and there were stains of blood and destruction. There were broken pieces of furniture, chewed wires, and papers everywhere. The rats had gotten into the test potions that gave you more strength and improved brain activity. There were hundreds of rats playing and fighting and toying with other animals. There were small rodents that were allies to the rats and wolves could stay if they committed to their cause. The ones that did not agree, well they were not around anymore. They had some beaver prisoners and had managed to get a bear to join their team. However, Kano the bear was just a cub and he was more playful than wanting to hurt anybody. He only did what the Rats said because they lied to him and told him they knew where his mother was and that they were friends.

Then I heard a voice, "Welcome to my party. I see that you have accepted my invitation and you must want to rule." I replied, "No, I don't want to rule. I just want the animals to be free." He replied, "No. No. No. The animals need to be ruled, and will be ruled by me, and by accepting this challenge I know you know this to be true. Whoever wins walks away as the King. Who doesn't want to be King? I know you do, and I know I do." He then began to sing and dance. He then sang, "Who wants to be King" and began to dance, telling us to keep up if we can. King Sunny

kept dancing and saying, "I have a speci

surprise for the winner so get to dancing." The

Rat King then yelled out, "Bring out the

prisoner!" Then appeared a battered and

bruised bunny being escorted by two rats and

it was Abir. I tried to hide my rage and

discomfort but that was a hard task to do. I

tried to move toward her but Uncle Leroy

grabbed me by the fur. Then the Rat King

looked at me in the eyes and I looked at him in

the eyes and glared. Then he said, "Let's get

ready for the dance off." We began to dance,

and Big Bucky and Tito were doing great

moves, but the Rat King's moves looked

superior to ours. He was shaking and flipping and doing moves that were creative with his hands and his feet. The animals were chanting, "Go Sunny!" and he was doing the same moves over and over.

Meanwhile with all the chaos going on in the Dulce, Dennis and Harry were approaching where Tito and Janus were in sector 15. Harry runs down the hall yelling, "I don't like confrontation!" He stops, hearing cries for help. Dennis was running down the hall behind him, and bumps into his back. Harry says, "Do you hear that noise? I hear someone calling for help over in that

direction." As they were walking towards the restricted area the lights were flickering. Then suddenly, out of nowhere, we see a beam of light. Lilly, Chad, and Hector appeared. They asked, "Where is Janus?" Harry replied, "He is in Sector 15, just down the hallway, and they need help, but will you help us free these animals first?" Chad offers his assistance, and opens all the cages. The animals start running down the hall, except one, a white and grey furred bunny. She asked, "Have any of you seen my son Ear-Z?" Harry replied, "Yes, he's in Sector 15. You can come with us, we are heading that way." Off they go back down the hall towards Sector 15.

Meanwhile back in Sector 15 things were getting tough in the dance off and King Sunny was showing his best moves. I looked at Tito, he looked back at me, and his whole body lit up and started glowing yellow and his moves were getting better and better. Then he moved to the front. As he was making his way to the front he touched Big Bucky and then me. We started to glow yellow, and our dancing improved. King Sunny's mouth dropped. He could not fathom how we were doing this. The Rats were astonished and in awe of what was happening. Then a beam of light brightens the room and Janus and Mascow Debucca appeared before us, along with Tania with ray guns pointed towards us. Meanwhile Dennis and Harry were leading Lilly, Chad, Hector, and Ear-Z's mother to Sector 15. Just before they arrived Lilly handed Dennis and Harry weapons and told Ear-Z's mom to wait by the door. Dennis and Harry had not used a weapon before and were excited and did not know how to use a weapon. Dennis accidently discharged his weapon. Up ahead within moments they were entering Sector 15. They entered the room and spotted Janus at pointing his Ray gun at Ear-Z and his friends.

Janus told Debucca, "grab Abir, this place is going to explode in ten minutes and good luck getting off this planet. Lilly, I am taking the ship and Abir!" Then Abir said, "Don't let him take me Ear-Z. Please help me!" Ear-Z replied, "I will never give up." Ear-Z grunted and tried to sprint towards Abir, but Janus, Debucca, and Tania beamed out of the room. Ear-Z yelled in rage and he swiped his hands through the air in displeasure. A voice on the loud speaker said, "Five minutes to self-destruction." We all began to run out on the Dulce Laboratories as fast as we could. I was happy that I helped save a lot of animals, but I thought about Abir and how Janus was treating her. I also thought about the animals I could not save while I was at the Dulce Laboratories. I grew up a lot, and I am forever changed, but my mission in life had only just begun. I knew I had to find Abir, and in order for me to do that I knew I would have to face Janus again. I will never stop fighting for Abir, I will not rest until she is safely back home. Now the training begins.

By Rashawn Epps

About the Author

Shawn K Epps born May 4, 1984- current.

Born in Salinas California. Facebook: Freeze

ORyan Prime

By Rashawn Epps